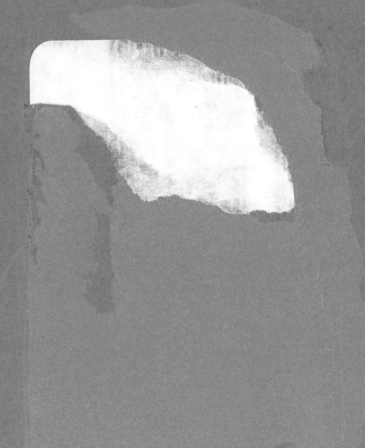

The Last Christmas Present

A Richard Jackson Book

The Last Christmas Present

by Matt Novak

Orchard Books   New York

Orchard Books, 95 Madison Avenue, New York, NY 10016

Manufactured in the United States of America
Printed by Barton Press, Inc. Bound by Horowitz/Rae
The text of this book is set in 20 point Zapf International Medium.
The illustrations are acrylic paintings reproduced in full color.
10   9   8   7   6   5   4   3   2   1

Library of Congress Cataloging-in-Publication Data
Novak, Matt. The last Christmas present / by Matt Novak.   p.   cm.
"A Richard Jackson book"—Half-title.
Summary: One of Santa's elves sets out on an adventurous journey to deliver a present that was accidentally left behind.
ISBN 0-531-05495-0.   ISBN 0-531-08645-3 (lib. bdg.)
1. Santa Claus—Juvenile fiction.   [1. Santa Claus—Fiction.
2. Christmas—Fiction.   3. Elves—Fiction.]   I. Title.
PZ7.N867Las   1993   [E]—dc20   92-44513

It was Christmas Eve at the North Pole.

Everyone was busy, especially Irwin.

The others were always telling him what to do.

After Santa had gone,

Irwin discovered something.

The big elves said,

"Our job is done, little one."

"We're on break, fruitcake."

"Just go to bed, chucklehead."

But Irwin could not sleep.

So he set out to deliver the present himself.

Hi, boy.

Mush.

He encountered many dangers.

Achoo.

Rumble

Avalanche!!

Grrr.

Thin Ice

Crack...

Uh-oh.

But finally he arrived

and found the right street

and the right house.

He sneaked inside,

and Santa let him put the present under the tree

all by himself.

Then they flew home,

where Santa thought of one last Christmas present.

And from that day on,

Irwin was the boss.

The end